An Elephant Family Adventure:
The Elephants in the Land of Enchantment

By

Beverly Eschberger

Books By Beverly Eschberger

Currently Available:

The Elephants Visit London
The Elephants Tour England
The Elephants in the Land of Enchantment

Other adventures with the Elephant Family soon to be published by Kinkajou Press:

The Elephants Visit the City of Light

Praise for the Elephant Family!

The Elephants Visit London

New Mexico Book Award Finalist, 2008

Midwest Book Review: The Elephants Visit London is a delightful and inexpensive treat for young readers who have just discovered the joy of chapter books. Following the Elephant Family (two parents and their twin children Harold and Penelope - all of the bipedal elephants dressed in nice travel clothes) during their trip to London. The Elephants Visit London shows an elephant's-eye view of historic buildings, traditional English food, and the Natural History Museum. But when the twins suddenly go missing from the museum, detectives from Scotland Yard are set on the case! The last few pages offer lists to help young readers reacquaint themselves with British English terms mentioned in the book, such as "telephone call box" (telephone booth). A scattering of simple black-and-white illustrations round out this wonderful book, fun to read in its own right and especially recommended to help prepare young people for the culture shock of visiting London and England.

Mom's Choice Awards ® Silver Award Winner: The Mom's Choice Awards® honors excellence in family-friendly media, products and services. An esteemed panel of judges includes education, media and other experts as well as parents, children, librarians, performing artists, producers, medical and business professionals, authors, scientists and others. Parents and educators look for the Mom's Choice Awards® seal in selecting quality materials and products for children and families. This book has been honored by this distinguished award.

The Elephants Tour England

Midwest Book Review: When you're a family of the world's largest land mammals, life isn't easy. "The Elephants Tour England" is a book aimed at first and second graders just beginning to read things slightly more difficult than picturebooks. Following a family of elephants as they tour England, it tells a story young readers will relish as they learn about the wonders of England and perhaps something of its neighbors. "The Elephants Tour England" is a fine choice for those catering to very young but adept readers.

ISBN13: 978-1-932926-02-6

Artemesia Publishing, LLC
9 Mockingbird Hill Rd
Tijeras, New Mexico 87059
info@artemesiapublishing.com
www.apbooks.net

Library of Congress Cataloging-in-Publication Data

Eschberger, Beverly Sue, 1968-
The Elephants in the land of enchantment / by Beverly Eschberger;
illustrated by Jim Gower.
     p. cm. -- (An Elephant family adventure)
Summary: Ambassador Elephant, Mrs. Elephant, and their children,
Harold and Penelope, visit their friend Maria in New Mexico,
where they enjoy the Albuquerque International Balloon Fiesta, a
quinceanera, and other special events.
   ISBN 978-1-932926-02-6 (pbk. : alk. paper)
  1. Albuquerque (N.M.)--Juvenile fiction. [1. Albuquerque (N.M.)--
Fiction. 2. Elephants--Fiction. 3. Hispanic Americans--Fiction.] I.
Gower, Jim, ill. II. Title.
  PZ7.E74465Ejl 2009
  [Fic]--dc22
                                   2009022011

First Printing

An Elephant Family Adventure: The Elephants in the Land of Enchantment

By

Beverly Eschberger

Illustrated By

Jim Gower

Kinkajou Press

Albuquerque, New Mexico

www.apbooks.net

To my son Christopher, who inspires me daily.

Table of Contents

Chapter One

A Letter from America

Once upon a time, a family of elephants lived in London. Mr. Elephant was the Ambassador to London from their home country of Elephas. Mrs. Elephant helped her husband to be the ambassador. She was also an artist who loved to paint and make statues.

Mr. and Mrs. Elephant had two children named Harold and Penelope. They went to school in London, where they had many friends.

Penelope was the smartest student in their class. She planned to be a paleontologist when she grew up.

Penelope loved to read books about dinosaurs

and other extinct animals. But she did not just like books about dinosaurs. She loved to read any book about any subject.

Harold was not as good a student as Penelope. He liked to spend his time playing games with his friends. His favorite games were those he made up with his toy soldiers.

Harold had a large collection of toy soldiers. He was always careful to save his pocket money. Then he could add new soldiers to his collection.

Harold wanted to be an astronaut when he grew up. Harold and Penelope's teacher was named Miss Wren. She often reminded Harold, "Now, Harold. You must study harder if you want to travel into space. You will need better grades in math and science."

One day, Mrs. Elephant opened a letter. "Oh, look," she said. "This is from one of my old students."

Before the family had moved to London, Mrs. Elephant was an art teacher. She had taught art classes at the Elephas University. She was an excellent teacher. And her classes were very popular with the students.

"Which one?" asked Mr. Elephant.

"Maria Gonzales," said Mrs. Elephant. "You remember her. She came to Elephas from the United States to study art."

"I remember her!" piped up Harold. She used to make yummy *empanadas*." He rubbed his stomach and smacked his lips.

"Oh, Harold," said Penelope. "You always remember food!"

"What is wrong with that?" asked Harold. "And she made *flan*, too!"

Mrs. Elephant continued reading her letter. "Maria says she is back in America. She lives in Albuquerque, New Mexico. Oh! How wonderful! She is going to have her first big art show. And she wants us to come see it!"

Harold and Penelope jumped up and down. "Yay!" cried Harold. "Can we please go? I want to see cowboys and Indians fighting!"

Mr. Elephant laughed. "I do not think you will see too many cowboys. Not in the city of Albuquerque. You might see some Native Americans. But they will not be fighting cowboys."

"But I want to see someone get scalped," said Harold.

"Oh, Harold. Do not say such horrible things," said Mrs. Elephant. "Nobody gets scalped anymore. At least, I hope not," she shuddered.

"Well, I want to see the dinosaurs," said Penelope. "The desert is a great place to find fossils."

"Dusty old bones," said Harold.

Penelope stuck out her tongue at him. "And the things the Native Americans left behind. Like stone carvings, pottery, and arrowheads."

"Arrowheads?" asked Harold. "If I can't see somebody get scalped, I'd like an arrowhead."

"It is settled then," said Mrs. Elephant. "I have always wanted to visit the American Southwest. The views are wonderful. I must pack extra paints and canvasses. Then I can paint some landscapes."

"What sort of art is Maria showing?" asked Mr. Elephant.

Mrs. Elephant read the letter again. "Hmmm, she does not say."

"What kind of art did she study?" asked Mr. Elephant.

"All different kinds," said Mrs. Elephant. "She took classes in drawing, painting, and making statues. She just could not make up her mind."

"Well, I guess we will find out in Albuquerque," said Mr. Elephant.

Mr. Elephant became serious. "Remember that elephants are not very common in America. People might become afraid if they see an elephant in New Mexico. So we must continue to wear our disguises."

In England, Mr. and Mrs. Elephant wore raincoats and carried umbrellas. Harold and Penelope wore school uniforms. When they wore their disguises, they looked like an ordinary English family.

Leaving London

On the day of their trip, the Elephants left the Elephas Embassy. They squeezed into a taxicab that took them to Heathrow Airport. On the way there, they pointed to their favorite sights.

"Look," said Harold. "There is Big Ben! Do you remember when we first came to London?"

"Yes," said Mr. Elephant. "You and Penelope were afraid you would not like it. You did not want to leave your friends in Elephas. Have you changed your minds?"

"Yes, Daddy!" said Harold and Penelope together.

"We love London. There are so many museums

here," said Penelope.

"And soldiers on horses!" said Harold. He pointed out the taxi window. One of the Queen's Guards was riding a horse.

At the airport, a porter loaded their suitcases onto a cart. He led the Elephants to the airline desk.

Mr. Elephant said, "I have tickets for four. The name is Elefant. E-L-E-F-A-N-T.

When Harold and Penelope had first heard this spelling, they were confused. Penelope had asked her father, "Daddy? Why did you spell our name Elefant with an F? Instead of with a PH?"

Her father had replied, "This is part of our disguise. What would people guess if they met a family named Elephant?"

Now, Harold and Penelope found it funny when their parents used this false spelling. It kept people from becoming suspicious that there were elephants around. They began to giggle, but Mrs. Elephant shushed them.

"Ah, yes, Mr. Elefant," said the desk clerk. "I have your tickets right here. I hope you have a wonderful visit to New Mexico."

"Thank you," said Mr. Elephant. "I am certain

we will." Mr. Elephant led his family to the first class area of the airplane.

The airplane soon took off. Harold and Penelope watched through the window. They saw the city of London disappear beneath their airplane.

"Look what I brought, Penelope," said Harold. He pulled some metal toys out of his pockets.

"More toy soldiers?" asked Penelope.

"No," said Harold. He held them up closer for her to see. "They are cowboys and Indians. Just like in the movies."

Mr. Elephant looked at Harold's toys. "I do not think you will see anyone who looks like that. Not many Native Americans carry bows and arrows. Or wear feathered headdresses. At least not everyday."

"I do not care," said Harold. "I still think they are fun."

Chapter Three

The Land of Enchantment

It was a long flight to New Mexico. When the airplane was landing, the Elephants looked out the windows.

"Look at the mountains!" said Penelope.

"The blue sky is so beautiful!" said Mrs. Elephant.

"Can you see any cowboys and Indians?" asked Harold.

After their airplane landed, the Elephants walked to the baggage claim.

Mrs. Elephant pointed to a statue. It was a Native American and eagle taking flight. "How lovely," she said. "The art in New Mexico is so different. It is giving me so many ideas already."

Mr. Elephant also pointed to the statue. "That is probably the only Native American you will see dressed like that." He said to Harold.

Harold said, "I know I will see someone wearing a headdress!"

The Elephants claimed their suitcases. They saw a familiar woman waiting for them.

"Look!" cried Penelope. "There is Maria!"

"I wonder if she brought any sweets," said Harold.

Harold and Penelope both ran to Maria. She gave them both big hugs. "My, my. You two are getting so big," she said.

"That is because I am 10 now," said Harold. He stood up straight and puffed out his chest. "Did you bring us any sweets?"

"You have not changed at all, Harold." Maria laughed. She pulled out a bag of skull-shaped candy. "I remember how much you like *calaveras de azucar*."

"Yummy!" cried Harold. He popped a candy into his mouth.

Maria added, "You are lucky it will soon be time for *El Día de los Muertos*. The Day of the Dead is the best time for skull candy."

Maria then hugged Mr. and Mrs. Elephant.

"It is so good to see you again," said Mrs. Elephant. "We have certainly missed your wonderful cooking."

"Yes," said Mr. Elephant. "I love the New Mexican foods you cooked. With the peppers and chiles. And the hot spices. We cannot find them in London."

"You must take plenty of peppers and chiles back to London," said Maria.

Maria took the Elephant family outside to her car. They all squeezed inside. Maria drove them to her house.

"Oh, the mountains are so beautiful!" cried Mrs. Elephant. "I am so glad that I brought extra canvasses. I can hardly wait to paint them."

"Those are the Sandia Mountains," said Maria.

"*Sandia* means "watermelon" in Spanish!" said Penelope. She had been studying Spanish for their trip.

"That is right," said Maria. "You will soon be speaking Spanish fluently."

"I hope so," said Penelope.

"We must go to Santa Fe while you are visiting," said Maria. "You will love the buttes even more. The shapes and colors of the rocks are amazing."

Harold suddenly pointed. "What is that over there? It looks like hot air balloons!"

"Yes," said Maria. "Albuquerque International Balloon Fiesta is this week. We will see many balloons. Sometimes they fly over my house."

"I have read about the Balloon Fiesta," said Mr. Elephant. "Albuquerque has the largest hot air balloon festival in the world."

"Wow!" said Harold. "Mummy, can we ride in a balloon?"

"Yes, Mummy," said Penelope. "It will be educational!" Penelope winked at Harold.

"Oh, dear," said Mrs. Elephant. She looked at Mr. Elephant. "I do not know about that."

They arrived at Maria's house. Many of her friends and family were waiting for them. They were cooking and making decorations.

Maria said, "We are having a big dinner tonight. It is to welcome you to Albuquerque. But we are also getting ready for a party tomorrow. My niece Alma is having her *quinceañera*.

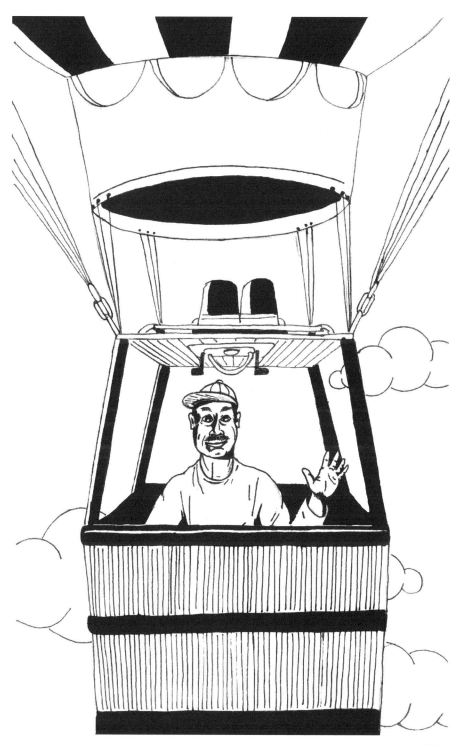

The Elephants were very confused. "What is a *quinceañera?*" asked Penelope.

"It is a very special party," said Maria. "When a Latina girl turns fifteen, we have a *quinceañera*. She is no longer a child. She is a woman. We have a party, and she gets special presents."

"That sounds like fun," said Penelope. "Mummy, can I have a *quinceañera* when I turn fifteen?"

Mrs. Elephant laughed. "We must learn more about it before we decide."

"What more is there to learn?" asked Penelope. "It is a party with presents. What else do you need to know?"

Maria became serious. "Oh, no. There is much more to a *quinceañera* than just the party. In New Mexico, it is very important. You will learn more at Alma's *quinceañera*."

Cooking

Maria took the Elephant family to their room. Bright wool rugs lay on the floor. And bright wool blankets covered the beds.

There were bright reds, yellows, greens and blues. The colors stood out against the white walls and dark wood floors.

Mrs. Elephant looked at some pottery on the dresser. "These are beautiful pieces, Maria. Did you make them?"

Maria blushed. "I made some of them. Others are very old. There have been many artists in my family. And we all like different types of art."

"That reminds me," said Mrs. Elephant. "Your letter did not say much about your art show. What kind of art will you be showing?"

Maria smiled, "That is a surprise. You will find out soon."

"Oh, please!" cried Penelope. She jumped up and down and clapped her hands. "Please tell us. Is it more pottery? What about some paintings? Maybe statues?"

Maria laughed. "I see you have not changed either, Penelope. No, you must wait. But I will tell you this much…" Penelope leaned forward, hoping to hear a big secret. "I think you will like it," said Maria.

Penelope was upset to not know what Maria's art was. She did not like it when people had secrets. Unless they told the secrets to her.

Maria left the Elephants to unpack their suitcases. They put away their clothes in the big, wooden dresser. Mr. and Mrs. Elephant hung up their raincoats in the closet.

Mr. Elephant gave them each a baseball hat to wear. "These hats will help us to fit in here," he said. "We would look very out of place wearing raincoats in the desert."

With their baseball hats, the Elephants looked like an ordinary American family.

Then they all went into the kitchen. Maria and several other women were cooking big pots of food.

Maria introduced them all by name. There were her mother, sisters, aunts and cousins. And the wives of her brothers. There were so many names to remember.

"And this is my *abuelita* MariCarmen," said Maria. "My grandmother. She is the most important person here."

"Wow," said Penelope. "You have a big family, Maria."

Maria laughed. "Family is very important to us in New Mexico. We like to have big parties whenever we can."

"I like parties, too," said Harold. "As long as there is food, I mean."

The women gave Harold and Penelope some cookies.

"Can I do anything to help?" asked Mrs. Elephant. She felt a little shy.

"Mrs. Elephant is a wonderful cook," said Maria. "She taught me all of the recipes I learned in Africa."

"Well, then, we can use her help," said Rosa. She was one of Maria's sisters. She handed Mrs. Elephant an apron and a spoon. She pointed to a pot.

Mrs. Elephant tied on the apron. It was embroidered with flowers and birds. She began to stir the pot.

Mr. Elephant cleared his throat. "Is there anything I can do to help?"

Rosa pointed to the door. "You can go help our husbands. They are cooking the meat for the party." She laughed. "They have the easy job." Maria and the other women laughed.

Mr. Elephant went outside. He found the men cooking different types of meat. They had beef, chicken, and pork. They were cooking everything on a big, open fire.

Harold and Penelope looked at each other. Penelope said, "I guess we are supposed to help, too."

Maria said, "No, you go outside and play with the other children." She shooed them outside.

Chapter Five

Elefant is Loco

It was late afternoon, but the air was still warm and dry.

Harold and Penelope saw a group of children. They were throwing a ball around.

Harold and Penelope went over to the children. "Hi," said Harold shyly. "I'm Harold Elefant. And this is my sister, Penelope."

"We are visiting from London," said Penelope.

"*Hola*," said one of the boys. "My name is Juan. Are there lots of elephants in London?"

"Um," said Penelope. "Well, there are some at the zoo… But I really would not know, uh. Since I've never, uh, seen an elephant in London."

"Oh, don't be silly," said another boy. "My name is Diego. And I can see that you two are elephants."

"Er, ah, no," said Harold. "We are not elephants. I just have a big nose."

"And big ears, too," said Penelope.

"No," said a girl. "We have all seen elephants at the zoo here. We know what an elephant looks like. Come and join us. My name is Eva."

"You mean you are not afraid?" asked Harold.

"You are not going to panic?" asked Penelope.

The children all shrugged their shoulders. "Why should we panic?" asked Juan. "Throw the ball over here, Carmen!"

While they were playing, a tall girl came outside. "Carmen, do not get your clothes dirty!" she called.

Carmen rolled her eyes. "That is my older sister, Alma. She thinks she is all grown up now. Because she is having her *quinceañera* tomorrow."

"I hope you will act like a young lady at my *quinceañera*. Your face is filthy. You are still such a tomboy," said Alma. "Who are your new friends?"

"These are Harold and Penelope Elefant," said Carmen. She winked at them. "They are visiting *Tía*

Maria from London."

"Elefant…Elefant…That is a strange name. It sounds pretty *loco* to me," said Alma. "I guess it is a British *gringo* name?"

"Um, yes. Yes it is," said Penelope.

Alma frowned in thought for a moment. "There is something strange about you two." She frowned again. "But I do not know what it is."

"Maybe it is because we are not American?" asked Harold.

"That must be it," said Alma. She frowned again. "I have always heard that British people had big noses."

"And big ears, too," piped up Penelope.

"Well, I have to get ready for my *quinceañera,*" said Alma. "It was nice to meet you." She went back inside the house.

"That was strange," said Penelope.

"She did not realize that we are elephants!" said Harold.

Carmen shrugged her shoulders. "I told you, she thinks she is all grown up. She cannot recognize an elephant now."

Chapter Six

Dinner and UFO's

When it was time to eat, everyone sat at big outside tables. Mr. Elephant carried a big platter of meat all by himself.

Maria's grandmother threw up her hands. "*¡Él es tan fuente!* He is so strong!" she cried.

Mr. Elephant put the big platter of meat on the table. Mrs. Elephant and the other women set big bowls of food on the table.

There were beans, *tortillas*, and meatballs called *albondigas*. There was a soup called *posole*. And a mix of vegetables called *calabacitas*. And big bowls of red and green chile sauce for everyone.

There was a big bowl of peas, just for the Elephant family. This pleased the Elephants, because (as everyone in London knows) elephants are very fond of peas.

Harold spooned large scoops of chile sauce onto his food. The rest of the family used much smaller amounts.

Mrs. Elephant waived her hand in front of her mouth. "Oh! I forgot how spicy the food is. *¡Muy caliente!*"

Mr. Elephant drank a tall glass of *cerveza*. "Spicy, but delicious!" he said.

Harold looked up from his plate. He popped a roasted green chile into his mouth. "What do you mean, spicy?"

Everyone laughed. Maria pointed at Harold's plate. "Look, Harold is having Christmas," she said.

"What?" asked Harold. He looked at his plate. "How can I be having Christmas? There is no plum pudding or Christmas goose?"

Maria laughed. "No, silly. In New Mexico, if you eat red and green chile sauce together, we say you are having Christmas. For the red and green colors.

"Oh!" said Harold. "I understand now!" He

began to eat hungrily. "Yum! This food is almost as good as Christmas."

For dessert, the women served *flan*.

After dinner, the children carried the plates into the kitchen. They stacked the plates next to the sink.

"We will wash them *mañana*," said Juan. He winked. "But only if my Mama makes us."

"Let's have some fun!" said Carmen.

The children ran into the yard. The sun was setting.

"Why don't we look for glow-worms?" asked Penelope. "I think you call them fireflies in the States."

Juan shook his head sadly. "We do not have fireflies in New Mexico."

"What?" asked Penelope. "What do you mean?"

"There are no fireflies in New Mexico," repeated Juan. "There just aren't any west of Kansas."

"Why didn't you know that, Penelope?" asked Harold. He was surprised.

Penelope was stunned. She had thought she knew everything about insects. "How can that be?"

"No one knows for certain," said Diego. He

shrugged.

"Our cousins who live in Texas see fireflies," added Carmen. "But we do not have any here."

Harold scratched his head. "Well, what do you do in the evenings? If you cannot look for glow-worms or fireflies?"

"We look for UFO's," said Diego. "You know, Unidentified Flying Objects."

"They usually come from the south," said Carmen. "Down by Roswell."

Harold and Penelope looked at Diego and Carmen. They did not know what to think.

"You are joking, right?" asked Penelope. She was not sure if they were telling her the truth.

"Sometimes they come from Area 51, in Nevada," added Diego. He grinned a little, trying not to laugh.

Penelope saw his grin. "Now I know you are teasing me," she said. She put her hands on her hips and smiled.

But Harold wondered if maybe they were not teasing. He looked up at the sky. Stars were starting to appear.

"I wonder if there are any UFO's out there tonight." Harold said this quietly, so no one could hear him.

Mrs. Elephant watched the sun set. It was bright orange. "*Que bonito*," she sighed.

"You see," said Maria. "You are speaking Spanish already."

"Only *un poco*." Mrs. Elephant laughed.

Maria's brothers and sisters brought out guitars. The family began to play music and sing Spanish songs. The children gathered around to listen.

Everyone played music until it was very late. Some of the younger children fell asleep in their parents' laps.

Harold and Penelope sat in Mr. and Mrs. Elephant's laps. They were still awake, but becoming sleepy.

Mr. Elephant felt sleepy from drinking *cerveza*. He was dozing in his chair.

Harold and Penelope felt their eyelids becoming heavy. They did not notice when Mrs. Elephant woke up Mr. Elephant.

Mr. Elephant picked up Harold. Mrs. Elephant picked up Penelope. They carried their children to the bedroom.

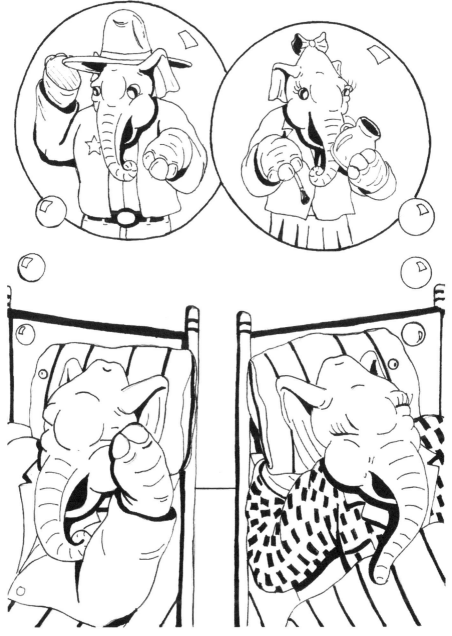

31

They tucked Harold and Penelope into their beds and kissed them goodnight. Then Mr. and Mrs. Elephant went to bed.

Mr. Elephant dreamed about delicious New Mexican food. He piled his plate high with spicy foods. Mrs. Elephant dreamed about painting beautiful landscapes. She used her brightest colors.

Penelope dreamed about being an archaeologist. She carefully dug up arrowheads and pieces of pottery.

And Harold dreamed about being a cowboy. He got to ride a horse and wear a cowboy hat. He carried a six-shooter and a lasso. Then he saw a group of Indians on horses.

The Indians wore feathered headdresses. They carried bows and arrows. Harold rode his horse over to them.

"Hey," said Harold. "Have you been rustling my cattle?"

The Indians just laughed at him. "Don't be silly," said one. "We don't do that anymore. Now, let's all go for a ride."

"Maybe we will find a UFO," said another. He laughed.

They rode their horses into the mountains.

Harold was happy to make new friends. (And he was glad they were not going to scalp him.)

Chapter Seven

Dawn Patrol

It was still dark the next morning when Maria woke up the Elephant family. They all yawned and stretched sleepily.

Maria made hot chocolate. They all ate a quick breakfast. Then they squeezed into Maria's car.

Harold yawned loudly. "Where are we going?" he asked sleepily.

"You will soon see," said Maria.

Maria parked her car in the dark. Other cars were parked there as well. She turned on a flashlight and led them onto a grassy field.

"This is a very strange place to be," said Mrs.

Elephant. "Are you sure we are in the right place?"

"Quite sure," said Maria. "Just follow me."

The Elephant family could hear and see people moving around. They were rustling fabric and moving things.

Suddenly a flame appeared near the Elephants. Harold and Penelope both screamed in fright. "Aaah! What was that?" cried Penelope.

"Is this a haunted house?" asked Harold.

"In the middle of a field?" asked Penelope.

"You will soon see," said Maria.

More flames appeared around the Elephants. And they could hear more people.

The light from the sun was peeking over the mountains. Its soft light fell on the large field. The Elephants could see large fluttering shapes. More and more flames began to appear. They made a loud, roaring sound.

"Where are we?" squeaked Penelope.

"What are these things around us?" Harold's voice shook.

"We are at the Albuquerque International Balloon Fiesta," said Maria. "We are here for Dawn Patrol."

"Dawn Patrol? What is that?" asked Harold.

Maria explained. "The Dawn Patrol are the first balloons to be launched. They let the other balloon pilots know which way the wind is blowing."

Maria continued, "We have what is called the Albuquerque Box. The winds blow in different directions at different heights. This means the balloons can circle around. They can stay in this area, instead of blowing away."

"There goes one now!" cried Harold. The Elephants could see a balloon lift off. It rose into the air. And began to float to the south.

The Elephants and Maria watched as more balloons lifted off. The balloons glowed as flames shot from their burners.

The sun rose higher. The Elephants could see the balloons more clearly. Then music began to play. Everyone became quiet.

"That is the United States National Anthem," said Maria. She pointed at a balloon as it began to rise. "There is our flag."

The Elephants could see the flag that hung from the balloon's basket. It flapped in the early morning breeze. The balloon turned slowly as it rose into the sky.

37

The National Anthem ended, and people clapped in excitement. Then more burners began to roar with flames. And more balloons began to launch. Soon the sky was filled with colorful balloons.

Harold and Penelope pointed to their favorite balloons.

"I like the one with the picture of the dragon," said Harold.

"I like the one with the hearts and flowers," Penelope said quietly.

"This would be so beautiful to paint," said Mrs. Elephant. "The morning light is so soft and pink."

Maria smiled. "Yes, I thought you would enjoy the balloons. We will see more of them later in the week."

The Elephants and Maria walked back to Maria's car. "Alma's *quinceañera* is tonight," said Maria. "It will be in a restaurant in Old Town. We can visit Old Town today before the party.

"What is Old Town?" asked Penelope.

"Penelope likes anything old and dusty," said Harold. Penelope stuck out her tongue at him.

"Well, Old Town is old. But it is not dusty," said

Maria. "Albuquerque was founded over three hundred years ago, in 1706. Old Town dates back to that time."

Maria continued, "I know that London is much, much older than that. Most European cities are thousands of years old. But that is very old for the United States. Old Town is made up of the original houses of Albuquerque. And there are science museums nearby," added Maria.

"That's what I want to see!" cried Penelope.

"And a rattlesnake museum," said Maria.

"Oh, dear!" gasped Mrs. Elephant.

"Yay!" cried Harold. "That's what I want to see! Cowboys and Indians and rattlesnakes!"

"I don't know if I want to see rattlesnakes," said Mrs. Elephant. She fluttered her hands in front of her face.

"Oh, but Mummy. It will be educational," said Harold. He winked at Penelope.

Chapter Eight

Visiting Old Town

Maria and the Elephant family drove to Old Town. They visited many shops. Mrs. Elephant bought gifts for their family in Elephas.

They saw people selling jewelry on blankets. Mrs. Elephant bought silver bracelets for herself and Penelope. The bracelets had turquoise stones set in them.

"These will be lovely memories of our visit," said Mrs. Elephant.

"And turquoise is the state gem of New Mexico!" added Penelope.

Maria laughed. "Penelope has a wealth of knowledge," she said.

"I do my best," said Penelope. She puffed out

her chest a little with pride.

"Oh, yeah?" asked Harold. "I know a state symbol that's more important than that."

"Oh, what is it?" asked Penelope. She did not believe that Harold could know more about New Mexico than she did.

"The state cookie is the *bizcochito*," said Harold. He stuck out his tongue at Penelope.

Penelope laughed. "Oh, Harold. You know everything about food."

"Well," said Harold. "It is a very important subject. At least it is to me."

Mr. Elephant patted Harold's shoulder. "It is to me as well, son," he said.

Harold continued. "I think other states should have state cookies, too. Or at least have a state dessert." He thought briefly. "New York could be cheesecake."

"That is a good idea, Harold," said Penelope. "England should have a national dessert, too."

"And what should the national dessert of England be?" asked Mrs. Elephant.

"Sticky toffee pudding!" cried both Harold and Penelope. They jumped up and down and clapped their hands.

"But we should also have a national cookie," said Penelope.

"Jammie Dodgers!" cried Harold.

"Mummy," Penelope asked. "Why do Americans call them cookies? Everyone in the British Commonwealth calls them biscuits."

"Enough!" cried Mr. Elephant. "All this talk about food is making me hungry! Let's have some lunch."

"An excellent idea, Mr. Elephant," said Maria. "And I know a wonderful café here. We can eat more traditional New Mexican foods."

Maria led them to an old building. "Church Street Café is the oldest house in Albuquerque. It was built by the early colonists," Maria added.

"Such a beautiful old building," said Mrs. Elephant.

"It must be sturdy, too," said Mr. Elephant. "It is three hundred years old."

"Do they serve good food?" asked Harold.

Maria laughed. "Yes, Harold. Very good New Mexican food."

It was a warm, sunny day. They sat at an outside table. The waiter brought *tortilla* chips and salsa.

Mrs. Elephant ordered *old fashioned chile rellenos.* Mr. Elephant ordered a *carne adovada al horno.* Penelope ordered *enchiladas.* Maria ordered the *handmade tamale plate.*

Harold ordered beef *fajitas.*

The waiter asked Harold, "*¿Salsa roja o verde?* Red or green sauce?"

Harold quickly replied, "*¡Navidad!* Christmas!"

They soon heard the sound of Harold's *fajitas* sizzling. Their food was served with *frijoles refritos* and Spanish rice.

The Elephants were sad that they were not served peas. Because (as it is known in New Mexico), Elephants are very fond of peas.

"Well," said Harold. "The *frijoles refritos* are almost as good as peas." He began to make his *fajitas.* He put the meat, onions, and bell peppers into the *tortillas.* Then he scooped sour cream, *guacamole, pico de gallo*, cheese, and tomatoes. He rolled it up, and took a big bite.

Maria and his parents watched Harold eat. "That is a lot of food just for you. Are you certain you can eat it all?" asked Mr. Elephant.

"Oh, yes," said Harold. "Can I have fried ice

cream for dessert?"

"Harold, you are an elephant, not a pig," said Penelope.

Harold trumpeted quietly. "All the fun today has made me hungry."

"Be sure to save some room for dinner tonight," said Maria. "We will have many special foods for the party."

"Will there be *bizcochitos*?" asked Harold.

"Of course," said Maria. "We always have *bizcochitos* for special events."

"Yay!" cried Harold. He finished his first *fajita*.

When they finished their meals, Harold and Penelope both ate fried ice cream for dessert. Harold rubbed his tummy. "Mmmm, that was good. But it is too bad they did not have any peas."

Maria said, "We do not cook with peas very often here. But we do like beans in many foods."

"Hmmm," said Harold. "I wonder what peas *refritos* would taste like."

"Yuck!" said Penelope. "That sounds awful. I will stick with *frijoles refritos* and regular peas."

"But Penelope," said Harold. "You never know. They might taste good. And you could add red and green chile sauce."

Penelope shook her head. "No, thank you!" she said.

Chapter Nine

The Quinceañera

After lunch, they continued to explore Old Town. Soon it was time for the *quinceañera.*

"As part of the *quinceañera,* we have a special mass. It is called the Mass of Thanksgiving. Or *la Misa de Accion de Gracias Quinceañera,*" said Maria. "I will explain to you what is happening."

Maria continued, "And do not worry. The mass will be in English, as well as Spanish."

"Whew!" said Harold. "That is a relief. I have enough trouble with French!"

"If you only paid attention in class," said Penelope. "Instead of playing with your toy soldiers."

"Maybe," said Harold. "But my soldiers are much more interesting." He pulled a toy soldier from his pocket.

Maria and the Elephants went inside the church. They sat down and waited for the mass to begin. The pews filled with other guests. No one noticed that there were elephants in the church.

Music began to play. Alma walked down the aisle. She wore a beautiful pink dress. She wore pink shoes with flat heels. She carried a doll in her arms. Behind her walked seven teenaged girls and seven teenaged boys.

Maria whispered to the Elephants. "You see the doll she is carrying? That is her *ultima muñeca*. It is her last doll."

The priest began to speak. "We are here for the *quinceañera* of Alma. Today she turns fifteen, she is *quince años*. Today she becomes a woman in the eyes of the church."

"We are here to give thanks to God for Alma's life. We have all watched her grow up. Today she tells God that she wants to follow him. She wants to be a good Christian woman. She will follow the teachings of God."

The priest continued, "Alma gives herself to God and the Virgin Mary today. Mary was also a young girl when God blessed her.

"Now Alma will show that she is putting away her childhood," said the priest. Alma's younger sister Carmen stood up. She wore a beautiful white lace dress. Alma gave her the *ultima muñeca*. Carmen sat down, holding the doll in her arms.

The priest continued, "She is now a woman." Alma's parents gave her a bunch of flowers. They put a crown on her head. Alma walked to the altar and placed her flowers on it. Her parents then gave her a scepter.

Maria was crying. She whispered to the Elephants again. "The *corona* and scepter show that Alma is a princess. A princess in the eyes of God."

Alma's godparents then stood up. They gave her a Bible, a crucifix, and a rosary. The priest blessed each gift.

The priest said, "I now present Miss Alma Gonzales. A new Christian woman." Alma had a big smile. Tears ran down her face because she was so happy.

As everyone left the church, Penelope was very

thoughtful. "Wow," she said. "There is lot that happens in a *quinceañera*."

"Yes," said Maria. "It is much more than just a big birthday party. It is a very important time in a girl's life."

"I'm not sure if want to have a *quinceañera* now. There is a lot to remember," said Penelope.

Chapter Ten

The Party

After the church service, everyone went to a nearby restaurant. This was where the party would be.

There were pink and white ribbons all over the restaurant. There was a dancing area with lights and a mirrored ball above it.

There were many long tables. Each table was covered with pink and white lace tablecloths. Everyone took a seat and waited for the food to be served.

The waiters soon brought big platters of food. They served *enchiladas, frijoles refritos,* and *calabacitas.*

Alma sat at the front table. She sat with her

parents and grandparents. The seven teenaged girls and seven teenaged boys sat with her as well.

Penelope asked Maria, "Who are the boys and girls sitting with Alma?"

"Those are the members of her court," Maria answered. She has seven *damas*, the girls. And seven *chambelanes*, the boys."

"Why seven? Is it a special number?" asked Penelope.

"Like lucky number seven?" asked Harold.

"It is simple," answered Maria. "Seven *damas*, plus seven *chambelanes*, plus Alma…"

"Equals fifteen!" said Penelope.

"Fifteen for the *quinceañera*," said Maria. "Fifteen years and fifteen people."

"I understand now," said Penelope. She frowned.

"What is the matter, dear?" asked Mrs. Elephant.

"I'm deciding who I want in my *quinceañera*. Hmmm, seven *damas* and seven *chambelanes*. This is going to be hard," said Penelope.

Harold rolled his eyes. "You should think more about what food you want. That is much more important."

Then an older man stood up. "I am Alma's *abuelito*, her grandfather. I remember the day when Alma was born. She was such a tiny baby. She was very sick." He sobbed.

"We were afraid that she would not live. We prayed and prayed for her to live. And God answered our prayers."

"Today Alma is still with us. She is strong and healthy. And today she has become a woman. Her *abuelita* and I are so proud of her."

Alma stood up and ran to her grandparents. She hugged and kissed them both. Tears were running down her face.

"Oh, that is so sweet," said Mrs. Elephant. She dabbed at her eyes with her large handkerchief. Penelope squeezed Mrs. Elephant's hand.

Alma sat down, still crying. Her grandfather held up a glass. "Please join me in thanking God for this wonderful day. And in praising my granddaughter for being so special."

Everyone raised his or her glasses in the toast.

More people stood up to toast Alma. They all

praised her. They talked about how beautiful and smart she was. They praised her for being a good Christian.

Then Alma's older brothers stood up. They told funny stories about when she was a little kid. Her brother Luis was telling a story about Alma being afraid of the dark.

"Enough!" said Alma, standing up. "I am a princess today. And if you tell any more stories about me, I'll, uh…"

"You'll what?" asked Luis.

"I won't invite you to my wedding!" Alma stuck out her tongue at him.

Everyone laughed. Alma's *abuelita* said, "Yes, she is quite the young lady today." Everyone laughed even harder.

Next the waiters brought in the cake. It was a large chocolate cake with white frosting.

"Wow," said Penelope. "It looks like a wedding cake." She watched as Alma and her parents cut the cake.

"Yes," said Maria. "A *quinceañera* is almost as important as a wedding. Today is Alma's special day." Maria sighed. "I remember my own *quinceañera*."

"What was it like?" asked Penelope.

"It was beautiful," said Maria. "It was like being a princess in a fairy tale. I had so much fun. And yes, we had wonderful food, Harold." Maria smiled. "I ate so much cake, I thought I would burst."

"That sounds like Harold's idea of a great party," said Penelope.

"That is right!" said Harold. He took a plate of cake from a waiter. "Mmmm, this is delicious!"

Chapter Eleven

Dancing

A band began to play a slow song. Alma's father stood up and took her hand. He carried a pair of pink, high-heeled shoes. He led her to a chair on the dance floor.

Alma sat in the chair, and her father knelt on the floor. Alma stretched out her feet to him. He took off her low-heeled shoes. Then he put the high-heeled shoes on her feet.

Alma's father then stood up. He held out his hand and helped Alma to stand.

Everyone clapped. Maria whispered, "The high-heeled shoes show that Alma is a woman now."

Next Alma and her father began to dance. Maria

added, "The *quinceañera* dances first with her father. Next she will dance with her *novio*, her boyfriend.

One of the *chambelanes* walked onto the dance floor. He bowed to Alma and her father. Alma's father bowed to him. Then the *chambelán* took Alma's hand. Alma and the *chambelán* began to dance.

Alma's father then went to where his wife was sitting. He bowed to her. She stood up and took his hand. Then they began to dance. Soon, other couples were on the floor dancing.

Mr. Elephant stood up and bowed to Mrs. Elephant. Mrs. Elephant dabbed at her eyes with her handkerchief. "Oh, this is so lovely," she sniffed. They tiptoed to the dance floor and began to dance.

Juan and Diego hurried over to Penelope. They were pushing each other. "Penelope," said Juan. "Would you like to dance with me?"

"No, dance with me!" said Diego.

Penelope smiled shyly. "I will dance first with Juan, because he asked first. Then I will dance with you, Diego."

"Yay!" said Juan. He punched Diego in the arm. Then he led Penelope to the dance floor. They began to dance. Juan whispered something in Penelope's ear. She blushed and giggled.

Diego turned to his aunt. "*Tía* Maria, would you like to dance?"

Maria smiled. "How kind of you to ask. Yes, I would like to dance very much."

Harold stayed at the table, eating cake. He looked up and saw Alma's sister Carmen. She was watching him. She smiled shyly.

Harold looked around. Was she smiling at him? Gulp! She must be. He took another bite of cake. Carmen smiled at him again.

Harold stood up and slowly walked over to Carmen. "Uh, hi, Carmen," he said, quietly. He looked at his feet.

"Hi, Harold," said Carmen.

Harold put his hand into his jacket pocket. He pulled out a squashed paper bag and opened it. "Would you like a Jelly Baby?"

"Oooh!" said Carmen, clapping her hands. "I love candy!" They each ate a Jelly Baby.

They stood quietly for a few minutes. Then Harold asked, "Um, do you want to dance?"

Carmen thought for a minute. Then she said,

"No. I cannot dance very well. Let's eat more cake instead."

Harold sighed. "Whew! That's a relief! I cannot dance very well either. But I love cake!"

"Me, too!" said Carmen. Let's go get some ice cream from the *cocina*."

"A great idea!" said Harold.

Harold and Carmen spent the rest of the party talking. They talked about their favorite foods. Especially their favorite sweets.

Harold promised to send Carmen Jelly Babies from London. Carmen promised to send Harold *calaveras de azucar* from New Mexico.

"Mmmm, I love sugar skulls, too," said Carmen.

Harold showed his toy soldiers to Carmen. He let her hold one of the Queen's Guards riding a horse.

Carmen blushed a little. "Alma teases me for being a tomboy. But I like playing with toy soldiers, too."

"Really?" asked Harold. He did not know what else to say.

Penelope danced with all the boys. She even danced with the older *chambelanes*. She was very light on her feet. During a break, she talked with Harold and

Carmen.

"All those dance classes have paid off," said Penelope. She fanned her face and took a sip of water. "You should come to dance class, Harold."

"No, thank you," said Harold. "I am happy just watching you." He smiled at Carmen, and she smiled back."

"Would you like some ice cream, Penelope?" asked Carmen.

Before Penelope could answer, Juan and Diego appeared.

"Penelope, the music is starting again. May I have this dance?" asked Juan.

"Me next!" said Diego.

Penelope blushed and giggled. She went to dance with Juan and Diego again.

Harold and Carmen just smiled at each other. Then they went back to eating their ice cream.

Chapter Twelve

The Art Piece

Maria woke the Elephants up early again the next morning. She made hot chocolate and breakfast *burritos*.

"Today is the first day of your art show?" asked Mrs. Elephant.

"Yes, it is," said Maria. She smiled.

"Are you going to tell us about your art? What sort of art will you be showing?" asked Mrs. Elephant.

"No," said Maria. "I want it to be a surprise."

"Can you give us a hint?" asked Penelope. She fidgeted in her seat.

"Hmmm, what can I tell you?" asked Maria. "It

is a large piece of art…"

"A statue!" blurted out Penelope.

"No. And it's very colorful," said Maria.

"A painting!" cried Harold.

"No. And it moves," said Maria.

Harold and Penelope both scratched their heads. "But artwork does not move," said Penelope.

"That is not true," said Mrs. Elephant. "You have seen statues that move."

"But Maria said it is not a statue," said Harold.

"That is right," said Maria. "Can you guess what it is?"

"A piece of pottery? A quilt? A rug?" asked Penelope. "Those are all things that can be art."

"That is right," said Maria. "But that is not what my artwork is."

"Is it food?" asked Harold.

"No," said Maria. She laughed.

"Then I give up," said Harold.

"Me, too," said Penelope.

"Well, you will soon see what it is," said Maria.

"Oh, I hate to wait!" said Penelope.

The Elephants and Maria squeezed into her car

again.

When Maria parked the car, Harold said, "Wait. This is where the Balloon Fiesta was."

"That is right," said Maria.

"But I thought we were here to see your artwork," said Mrs. Elephant.

"We are," said Maria. "Follow me." She turned on her flashlight and led them out onto the grassy field.

The Dawn Patrol balloons had already launched. They glowed above the field. The Elephants could see and hear flames on the field. Other balloons were getting ready to launch.

"Just look over here." Maria led them to a large pile of fabric.

"Good morning," said a man with a deep voice. "I am the pilot." He shook hands with Mr. and Mrs. Elephant.

"Pilot?" Harold scratched his head. "Where is your airplane?"

The man laughed. "No, I am the balloon pilot. It is time to get this balloon ready. You can help us."

Mr. Elephant and the pilot lifted a basket out of a truck. Maria and the pilot hooked ropes to the basket.

Then they hooked the ropes to the fabric.

Maria and the pilot turned on fans. The fabric began to puff up with air.

"Now stand back a little," said the pilot. Flames shot from a burner at the top of the basket. It roared loudly.

Harold and Penelope both squealed. They grabbed their parents' hands. The pilot kept the fire burning. Maria shook out the fabric as it filled with hot air.

"Look!" cried Harold. "What is wrong with it? Hot air balloons are supposed to be round!"

"Sometimes they are," said the pilot.

"But they can be other shapes, too," said Maria.

"My goodness," said Mrs. Elephant. "Look at that! Is it…is it…?"

"An elephant!" cried the Elephant family together.

"No, wait!" said Mr. Elephant. "It's…"

"Four elephants!" they all cried.

"Yes," said Maria. "The time I studied art in Elephas was wonderful. You and the other elephants were so kind. I created this balloon to remember Elephas." She gave each of the Elephants a big hug.

"Oh, that is so sweet!" Mrs. Elephant dabbed at her eyes with her handkerchief.

"I am so proud that our country meant so much to you," said Mr. Elephant.

"Wow!" said Harold and Penelope. They ran around the balloon.

"Look!" cried Harold. "There is the flag of Elephas."

"And the Great Seal of Elephas," said Penelope.

"Would you like to ride in it?" asked the pilot. "Or watch from the ground?"

The Elephants all thought for a moment. "We will ride in it!" shouted Harold and Penelope.

"We will watch from the ground," said Mr. and Mrs. Elephant.

Harold and Penelope climbed into the basket. Maria and the pilot climbed in, too.

A man dressed in black and white blew a whistle. The pilot turned on the flames again.

The balloon began to rise. Harold and Penelope waved to their parents on the ground.

"Be careful!" called Mrs. Elephant. She sounded worried, but happy.

Harold and Penelope saw people pointing at the

69

balloon.

"Look there," said a man. "A balloon with *four* elephants!"

"That is a new balloon for this year," said a woman.

"That is the creator of the balloon in the basket. But who is that with her? The kids with the big noses?" asked the man.

"We're from Elephas!" shouted Penelope.

"And we are proud to be elephants!" called Harold.

"What did he say?" asked the woman.

"Something about a lamppost?" That makes no sense," said the man.

Harold and Penelope continued to wave as the balloon rose. They could see other balloons begin to take off.

"Wow!" said Harold. Look at all the different shaped balloons! I see a cow and a fish!"

"Look at the bees! They are kissing!" cried Penelope.

"I never knew that balloons could have so many different shapes." Harold scratched his head.

"The wind is taking us to the north today," said

Maria. "The chase crew will bring your parents to meet us when we land."

"This is wonderful," said Penelope. "I never want to land!"

"Forget being an astronaut," cried Harold. "I want to be a balloon pilot!"

"If we don't land, we will miss the balloon party tonight. And the food," said the pilot.

"Will there be *bizcochitos*?" asked Harold.

"And peas?" asked Penelope.

"Of course," said Maria.

This pleased Harold and Penelope. Because (as everyone in New Mexico knows), elephants are very found of peas.

Fun Facts about New Mexico

Capital City	Santa Fe
Largest City	Albuquerque
Became a State	January 16th, 1912 (47th State)
State Motto	*Crescit eundo* – Latin ("It Grows as It Goes")
State Nickname	"Land of Enchantment" (*"Tierra del Encanto"* – Spanish)
State Flower	Yucca flower
State Bird	Greater Roadrunner
State Animal	Black Bear
State Vegetables	*Frijoles con chile* (Beans and chiles)
State Gem	Turquoise
State Fossil	Coelophysis
State Cookie	*Bizcochito*
State Insect	Tarantula Wasp
State Question	"Red or green?" (For red or green chile.)
State Flag (red Zia sun symbol on yellow)	

The Elephants' Guide to Speaking Spanish

El Día de los Muertos = The Day of the Dead. It is celebrated November 1st and 2nd. These are the Catholic holy days of All Saint's Day and All Soul's Day. October 31st (Halloween) is All Hallows' Eve.

Sandia = watermelon

Mesa = table, or a rock formation with a flat top

Quinceañera = a special party held when a Latina girl turns fifteen

Abuelita = grandmother

Hola = hello

Tía = aunt

Loco = crazy

Gringo = foreigner

"¡*Él es tan fuente!* = He is so strong!

¡Muy caliente! = Very hot!

Mañana = tomorrow

Que bonito! = How beautiful!

Un poco = a little

¿Salsa roja o verde? = Red or green sauce?

Navidad = Christmas

Ultima muñeca = last doll

Corona = crown or tiara

Dama = lady

Chambelán = escort

Abuelito = grandfather

Novio = boyfriend

Cocina = kitchen

The Elephants' Guide to New Mexican Food

Empanada = a stuffed pastry

Flan = a caramel custard

Calaveras de azucar = a candy in the shape of a human skull. They are usually eaten around Halloween or *El Día de los Muertos* (The Day of the Dead).

Chile or *Chile pepper* = small, hot peppers (sometimes spelled *chili* or *chilli*)

Albóndigas = meatballs made with rice

Calabacitas = a mix of onion, zucchini, yellow squash, tomatoes, green chile, cilantro, oregano, and cloves

Tortilla = a round, flat bread made with corn or wheat flour

Salsa = sauce, usually a hot sauce

Cerveza = beer

Bizcochito = a crispy butter cookie, flavored with anise and cinnamon

Carne Adovada al Hondo = pork marinated in red chile and wrapped in a large flour tortilla

Chile rellenos = chile peppers stuffed with cheese and fried

Enchiladas = small corn tortillas that are filled, rolled up, and cooked in an oven

Tamales = steam cooked corn flour dough, sometimes

with meat, wrapped in a corn husk

Fajitas = grilled meat, onions, and peppers, served on a tortilla

Frijoles refritos = refried beans

Guacamole = mashed avocado with tomatoes and salt

Pico de gallo = "rooster's beak"; chopped tomatoes, onions, and jalapenos or serranos

Fried ice cream = ice cream rolled in cookie crumbs and deep fried in cooking oil

Breakfast *burritos* = a large flour tortilla filled with scrambled eggs, potatoes, sausage, onions, peppers, and chile sauce

The Elephants' Guide to British Terms and British Food

Pocket money = allowance

Sweet = candy

Sticky toffee pudding = sponge cake made with dates and covered with toffee sauce

Jammie Dodger = a British sandwich cookie with a jam filling

Biscuit = cookie

Jelly Baby = a soft candy, they come in different colors and fruit flavors

Help the Elephants Plan Their Next Vacation!

Where would you like to see the Elephant family visit next?

Please email the Elephant Family at:
elephants@simplyelephants.com
(Always get your parents' permission before going online!)

Or send a post card to:
The Elephant Family
Kinkajou Press
9 Mockingbird Hill Rd
Tijeras, NM 87059

You can learn more about the Elephant Family and their adventures at: www.simplyelephants.com

Dear Elephant Family,

I would like to see you visit _____

_____

_____

I think that you would have fun there because _____

_____

_____

_____

Things that I liked about your adventures in Albuquerque

were _____

_____

_____

Your friend, _____

_____

_____

Free Elephant Family Fan Club

Want to keep up with all of the Elephant Family's Adventures? Join the free Elephant Family Fan Club!

See where the Elephants are traveling to next. Register for e-mail greetings from Harold and Penelope, and more! Be the first to find out about the next Elephant Family Adventure book. Buy Elephant Family books and gifts.

All new fan club members will receive a free gift from the Elephant Family.

Sign up online at www.simplyelephants.com
(Always get your parents' permission before going on-line!)
Or send a postcard: Elephant Fan Club
Kinkajou Press
9 Mockingbird Hill Rd
Tijeras, NM 87059

Coming Soon!

The Elephants Visit the City of Light

An adventure in Paris! Mr. Elephant has been invited to Paris for an important diplomatic meeting.

Harold and Penelope are looking forward to visiting their French friends. And all of the Elephants want to eat French food.

But what happens when Mr. and Mrs. Elephant disappear in Paris? Will Harold and Penelope have to stay in Paris and learn French? And will Harold be arrested for climbing on an important monument?

Get ready for a great adventure with the Elephant family!

Beverly Eschberger enjoys writing the sort of books that she would have liked to read as a child. These books include *The Elephants* series, and several other books soon to be published.

Ms. Eschberger lives in New Mexico, with her husband Geoff and son Christopher. She has volunteered at the Albuquerque International Balloon Fiesta for the past two years. When she does not have her nose buried in a book, she enjoys writing about paleontology, nature, and travel.

Order Form
Elephant Family Adventures

_____ The Elephants Visit London ($3.99 ea.)
_____ The Elephants Tour England ($3.99 ea.)
_____ The Elephants in the Land of Enchantment ($3.99 ea.)
_____ The Elephants Visit the City of Light ($3.99 ea.)
        (forthcoming)

_____ Total Number of Books _____ Total Cost
_____ I would like my copy autographed by Beverly
        Eschberger!

My Check or Money Order for $ _____ is enclosed.
Please charge my _____ Visa _____ MC

Name: _____

Address: _____

City: _____

State: _____ Zip: _____

Email: _____

Phone: _____

Credit Card #: _____

Exp Date: _____ CCV# _____
                            (3 digit # on back of card)

Mail to: Artemesia Publishing
         9 Mockingbird Hill Rd
         Tijeras, New Mexico 87059
Or Call: 1-505-286-0892